W9-AVO-797

Stella Batts
Broken Birthday

Stella Batts

Broken Birthday

Book

Courtney Sheinmel

Illustrated by Jennifer A. Bell

To brave kids everywhere, especially Rachael Rose and Daniel Gregory
—Courtney

Sleeping Bear Press™

2395 South Huron Parkway, Suite 200, Ann Arbor, MI 48104
www.sleepingbearpress.com
© Sleeping Bear Press

TWIZZLERS is a registered trademark of Hershey Chocolate & Confectionery Corporation. Peachie
O's is owned by Trolli, a registered trademark and company owned by the Ferrara Candy Company.
iPad® and FaceTime® are registered trademarks of Apple Inc. Swedish Fish® is a registered
trademark of Cadbury Adams USA LLC.

Printed and bound in the United States.
10 9 8 7 6 5 4 3 2 1

Library of Congress Cataloging-in-Publication Data • Names: Sheinmel, Courtney, author. • Bell,
Jennifer A., illustrator. • Title: Broken birthday • written by Courtney Sheinmel ; illustrated by
Jennifer A. Bell. • Description: Ann Arbor, MI : Sleeping Bear Press, [2017] • Series: Stella Batts;
book 10 • Summary: "Stella and her family have special plans to celebrate her ninth birthday
but everything changes when Stella falls and breaks her leg at school"— Provided by publisher.
• Identifiers: LCCN 2016026744 • ISBN 9781585369218 (hard cover) • ISBN 9781585369225
(paper back) • Subjects: | CYAC: Fractures—Fiction. | Friendship—Fiction. • Birthdays—Fiction.
• Family life—Fiction. • Classification: LCC PZ7.S54124 Bro 2017 • DDC [Fic]—dc23 • LC record
available at https://lccn.loc.gov/2016026744

Table of Contents

Things I Wrote About When I Was Eight 7

Closer to Nine 11

My Birthday Observed 25

More Bad Things 41

All of a Sudden 57

The Signal 71

The Recovery Room 79

Out With a Smash 87

Officially Nine 105

Happy Birthday 123

My Birthday Wish 137

CHAPTER 1

Things I Wrote About When I Was Eight

Hi, it's Stella Batts again!

I've written nine books since I turned eight years old. That's because a lot of things happened to me that I wanted to write about, such as:

1. Joshua in my class started calling me Smella, so I changed my name. But then I changed it back again.

2. I taste-tested magic gum, which was fun.

But then I got it stuck in my hair, which was NOT fun at all. Plus, my best friend Willa moved away, which was the most not-fun thing ever.

3. But I got a new best friend, named Evie, who moved here from London. She has a cool accent.

4. My baby brother, Marco, was born.

5. I got to babysit Evie's dog, and I lost it! Luckily, my sister, Penny, helped find it.

6. Penny and I were flower girls, we got a new uncle and a new cousin, and we all went swimming in our flower-girl dresses!

7. My friend Lucy and I made a secret newspaper. I wrote about the secret new Candy Carnival at our store, Batts Confections. (It's not a secret anymore.)

8. I got to be on my favorite show in the whole entire world, called *Superstar Sam*.

I slept over in my school library.

In this book I'm going to write about the amazing trip my family and I are about to take. And guess what? By the time I finish this book, the other thing that will have happened is I will have turned NINE YEARS OLD!

CHAPTER 2

Closer to Nine

"Stella, there's a phone call for you," Mom said.

I love getting phone calls!

"Hello, this is Stella Batts," I said, pressing the phone against my ear. "Who is this?"

Next to me, my sister, Penny, whined in my other ear. "How come I didn't get a phone call?"

"Shhh, Penny, I can't hear," I said. "Who is this?" I asked again.

"Guess," said a voice on the other end of

the phone.

"Willa!" I nearly screamed. "Of course I know who it is! You're my best friend! I can't wait to see you in person! It will be my best birthday EVER!"

"Me toooooo!!!!" Penny cried, leaning toward the phone.

"It's not going to be your birthday," I told her.

"I mean I can't wait to see Willa, too!" she said. "WILLA!!!!"

"Inside voices, girls," Mom said. "Please."

"Let me talk to Willa," Penny said, in a soft inside voice.

"No," I told her, in my soft inside voice.

"I don't mind if Penny wants to talk to me," Willa said.

Willa is very nice. As a matter of fact, she's the nicest person I've ever met in my whole entire life! But I knew she'd called to talk to me, not Penny.

"It's not fair," Penny told Mom.

"Hold on," I said into the phone. I walked out of the kitchen, down the hall, and into my room.

"You know what's weird?" I asked Willa. "You know exactly what my house looks like. But when you walk in yours, I have no idea what it looks like."

"You'll know in two more days," Willa said.

"I know!" I said. "I'm so excited!"

If you haven't guessed already, that was the amazing trip I mentioned in Chapter One—a trip to Willa's house in Pennsylvania. From Saturday morning until Tuesday night—four days and three nights!

"I'm more excited," Willa said.

"And I'm the MOST excited," I told her. "I'm so excited I feel like . . . I feel like I could hug the whole entire world. That's how excited I am. And the best part is, it'll be my birthday when I'm there."

"A sleepover birthday," she said. "My mom and I planned it all out. You and Penny will sleep in my room, and your parents and Marco will sleep in Jackson's room."

"With Jackson?" I asked. Jackson is Willa's younger brother.

"Jackson is going to sleep in Spencer's room," Willa said. Spencer is her older brother. "My mom said it's like musical beds."

"That's funny," I told her.

"So, what are you doing between now and when you get here?" Willa asked.

"Right now we're making cupcakes for my party at school tomorrow," I told her. "We can't frost them yet, because we're waiting for my dad to come home from the store with all the toppings. There's going to be rainbow sprinkles, chocolate sprinkles, chocolate chips, cubes of fudge, and probably a million more things."

"A million? Really?"

"No, not a million. But a lot. As soon as he gets here, we'll decorate the cupcakes. Then I'll go to sleep, and wake up and go to school, and have my party. Then after that, Mom will pick me and Penny up. We'll go to sleep one more time and when we wake up it'll be time to go visit you."

"Do you know what I'm doing?" Willa asked.

"No, what?"

"I'm making you a friendship bracelet."

"Is that my present?" I asked.

Some people like their presents to be surprises, but I like to know because then I can be happy about whatever is going to happen for even longer.

"You'll see," Willa said in a teasing voice.

"But I—" I started.

Just then Willa's mom said something to her in the background, and Willa said, "Stella, my mom says I have to hang up now because it's almost my bedtime."

"What?" I said. "It's not even six o'clock."

"It's three hours later in Pennsylvania," she reminded me.

"Oh yeah."

"Got to go," she said. "I'll see you in two days. Tell Penny I'm sorry I didn't talk to her, but I'll see her, too!"

"Bye, Willa," I said.

After we hung up, Dad still wasn't home, so I decided to pack for the trip. I've had a lot of experience packing, because I'd helped Mom pack my bag for Aunt Laura's wedding, and I'd practically packed by myself to go on my school library sleepover.

This was a bigger trip, so packing was even more important. I pulled things from my closet, my dresser, and my desk, and made a big pile of stuff on the floor.

Someone knocked on my door. I have a sign posted that says *This is Stella's Room. If*

You Are Not Stella Then Please Knock. Penny never reads the sign. Marco doesn't know how to read. So the person knocking had to be Mom.

"Come in," I told her.

She did, along with Penny and Marco. Mom and Penny walked, of course. Marco crawled. It's his new trick. He's getting pretty good at it. Mom and Dad made a rule that Penny and I had to keep things clean from now on. It was always the rule, but now they are SUPER strict about it, because whatever gets left on the floor, Marco pops into his mouth to eat. Books, pens, pen caps, socks, my Glinda the Good Witch Wand, Penny's favorite stuffed animal Belinda. You name it, Marco will try to eat it.

Mom scooped Marco up quick as a wink when she saw everything piled on my floor.

"Stella, what on earth is happening in here?"

"It's okay," I told her. "I'm not breaking any rules. I'm just packing."

"It looks like you're packing to go away for a month," she said. "I don't think you need a dozen shirts for a long weekend in Pennsylvania."

"Only eleven," I told her.

"And your flower-girl dress from Aunt Laura's wedding?" she asked.

"I thought I might need something fancy for my birthday," I explained. "That dress is the fanciest thing I've got."

"I'll get my dress, too!" Penny said, and she moved toward the door.

"Not so fast," Mom told her.

"That's right," I said. "It's my birthday, so I should wear the fanciest thing."

"It's not fair," Penny said again, pouting.

"Stella Rae," Mom said, shaking her head. She sat down on my bed with Marco in her arms. "We really need to pare down this pile."

"I know what *pair* means," I told her. "And I know what *down* means. But what does *pair down* mean?"

"It's P-A-R-E down," she said.

"Ooh, goody," I said. "A new word!"

I love new words. I like to put at least one new word in every book I write, and sometimes even more than that.

"What do you think it means?" Mom asked me.

"It means you want me to bring less."

"Exactly. Now, put everything away, and I'll pack for you later."

"I'm old enough to pack myself," I told her. "After all, I'm nine."

"You're *eight*," Penny said.

"I'm afraid she's right, for a few more days at least, my sweets," Mom said.

"I'm closer to nine than I am to eight. I'm only three days away from nine, but my eighth birthday was . . . three hundred and sixty-two days ago."

"One day you won't want to be any older," Mom said.

"Sure I will."

"No, you won't. Trust me."

Grown-ups always think they'll know what kids will want when they're older. But I had a feeling Mom was wrong about me. I loved getting older—especially since it meant I got to have a birthday.

"I don't want to be any older," Penny said. She dropped to the floor and rolled around a bit. "Goo goo gaga. I'm a baby. I can't even crawl. I'm younger than Marco now!"

"Penny, get up," Mom said. "You're a big kindergarten girl—and that's way more exciting than being a baby. Think about all the things you can do!"

"You just said getting older was a bad thing," I reminded Mom.

"I said there was no reason to rush it along," Mom said.

"Goo goo gaga," Penny said, rolling around again. "Goo goo ga ga ga. Ooh, I can feel the garage opening!"

"How'd you feel that?" I asked.

"The floor vibrated," she said, as she sprang to her feet. "Daddy's home! The toppings are home!"

"Yay!" I said.

Marco clapped his hands.

"What took him so long?" Penny asked.

"He had to work," Mom said. "You know

that. Stuart hasn't been around as much."

Stuart is my favorite person who works at Batts Confections.

"Why not?" I asked.

"Because he's graduating college in a few weeks," Mom said. "And he's getting ready to move to New York."

"He's leaving us?" I asked.

"I'm afraid so," Mom said.

"I hate when people move away," I told her.

"I know," she said. "But now we'll have another person to visit on the East Coast." She looked down at my pile of clothes on the floor. "Tell you what, my nearly nine-year-old girl. I'll give you an early birthday present right now. You can wait on cleaning up, as long as you promise to do it after cupcakes."

"I promise," I said. "Thanks, Mom."

CHAPTER 3

My Birthday Observed

The next day, Dad drove our carpool to school. Here's who was in our car:

1. Dad, of course
2. Me and Penny
3. My friend Evie
4. Penny's friend Zoey

"Happy birthday," Evie said to me when she got into the car.

"It's not really her birthday yet," Penny told her.

"I know that," Evie said. "I'm her best friend after all."

"Well," I said. "Willa's actually my best friend, but she moved away. So you're my best friend who lives in Somers."

"Hey, Stella," Dad said.

"What?"

"Nothing. We'll talk later. How about some car tunes?"

"Yay! Car tunes!" Penny said. "Put on the show tunes channel!"

Penny likes show tunes because that's what our Grandma Dee listens to.

"What was that?" Dad said. "I think I heard a question . . . but I'm not sure. Something was missing."

"PLEASE!" Penny added.

"Well, in that case," Dad said, and he flipped on the radio. "Here you go."

But I was almost nine, so I knew Dad had only mentioned car tunes because he wanted to distract me. That trick always works on Penny, because she's only five. I'm too old to be easily distracted.

"What do we have to talk about later, Dad?" I asked.

"Not now, Stel," he said. "This is my favorite song." And he turned the volume up.

"I don't like this song," I said.

"All right, Stel," Dad said, changing the station. "How about this one?"

"Better," I said.

"But I liked the other song better," Penny said. "It's not fair."

"Sure it is," I told her. "It's MY birthday."

"Not for two more days," Penny corrected.

"You don't always celebrate your birthday on your birthday," I said. "It's like how we have
- President's Day *Observed* off from school. I wonder if I'll get any presents today."

"Oh no," Evie said. "I didn't bring one for you."

"That's okay," I told her. "There are still more days. But you want to know one of the things that Willa is giving me? A friendship bracelet! Because we're best friends!"

"I love friendship bracelets," Evie said. "I made them for Sara and Tesa in London. I'll make one for you, too."

"That's okay," I told her. "I don't need it. I'll have Willa's."

"You can never have too many friendship bracelets," Dad said.

"You don't have any!" Penny squealed.

"That's because I'm not in school

anymore," Dad said. "But speaking of school—here we are."

He pulled up in front of the big sign that says SOMERS ELEMENTARY SCHOOL.

"All right, everyone," Dad said. "Up and out. Stella, Mom and I will see you after lunch."

"And you'll see me, too, right?" Penny said.

"I'll see you after that," Dad said. "When you come home from school."

"It's not fair that you see Stella more times than you see me," Penny told Dad.

"I'll see you after lunch during school when it's your birthday," Dad said.

He'd still see me more times than he'd see Penny, because I'm three years older, and I'll always have three more years of time than she did. I would've told her that, but Evie pulled on my arm and said she didn't want to be late.

Then Dad said he didn't want Penny and Zoey to be late, either. So we said good-bye and got out of the car.

Penny and her friend Zoey went to their classroom, and Evie and I went to ours. Our teacher, Mrs. Finkel, was standing at the front of the room. She clapped her hands to signal that it was time to get started with our day. We did some math work, and then some social studies.

If it was a normal day, after social studies we'd take a break for snack. But since it was My Birthday Observed, it wasn't a normal day. We skipped snack time.

"Boo!" Joshua shouted when Mrs. Finkel announced that we'd be opening our science textbooks instead.

"No Calling Out is a Ground Rule," Mrs. Finkel reminded him. "But if you want to visit Principal O'Neil's office, I'm sure he'd be happy to have you this afternoon while the rest of us celebrate Stella's birthday."

Joshua didn't call out again after that. None of us did. After our morning lessons it was time for lunch, and then recess.

Usually lunch and recess are my two favorite parts of the day. But on My Birthday Observed they went by so slowly. SOOOOOOOO SLOOOOOOOWLY. That's what happens when you're waiting for something good to happen. It's like being at Batts Confections and waiting for the homemade fudge to cool. Dad says it takes three to four hours, but trust me when I say it feels more like three to four DAYS.

We had more lessons after recess was over, and time went even slower. So slowly it practically felt like it had stopped. Finally there was a knock on the classroom door.

"All right, everyone," Mrs. Finkel said. "You can put your books in your desk."

She went to the door to open it. Can you guess who walked in? If you said my mom, then you are EXACTLY RIGHT.

Mom was carrying two big boxes, which I knew had the cupcakes inside them. I wanted to run up and say hello. But since I was in school, and Mrs. Finkel was there, it was hard to know who was in charge. I raised my hand first.

"You can go ahead and say hello to your mother, Stella," Mrs. Finkel said.

"Hi, Mom," I said. "Where's Dad?"

"He had to stay at work," Mom said. "He's very sorry, but he has to make sure everything at the store is in order before the trip." I felt a little bit sad, but then Mom added, "Come on

now, we've got cupcakes to hand out."

Except it wasn't time to hand them out just yet. First Mrs. Finkel told the class to sing to me. I stood next to Mom, while everyone sang the happy birthday song. It made my cheeks get warmed up, like when you're embarrassed and they turn the color of pink cotton candy. I don't know why I was embarrassed, since everyone was looking at me for a good reason. But that's how I felt. Afterwards I said, "Thank you," in a shy voice, like the way my friend Arielle's voice is.

"Happy birthday to you, happy birthday to you, you look like a monkey, and you smell like one too!" Joshua called out.

"Joshua!" Mrs. Finkel said. "One more outburst and you'll spend some quality time with Mr. O'Neil—WITHOUT a cupcake."

Then Mrs. Finkel told me to pick two volunteers to help pass out paper plates and napkins. Joshua raised his hand. "Ooh ooh ooh, pick me!" he said. But I didn't because he wasn't acting like my friend right then, and I had lots of other friends to choose from.

It's hard to pick only two friends to volunteer when you have more than that. I picked

Evie, and then I did eeny meeny miny moe to pick the next person, which was Lucy.

Evie and Lucy gave everyone plates and napkins. Mom and I followed behind them and gave out the cupcakes. Everyone loved what they looked like. Even Joshua said they were the best-looking cupcakes he'd ever seen.

"Mine has a mountain of candy on it!" he said.

"So does mine," said Eleanor.

"And mine too," called Clark.

Evie, Lucy, and I were back at our seats. Mrs. Finkel didn't tell us to be quiet again, because it was kind of like snack time, even though it was after lunch instead of before. I explained to everyone how Penny and I had made the cupcakes look so good. First we'd made vanilla frosting, and we'd mixed in food coloring, so some cupcakes were frosted pink, some green, and, of course, yellow and blue, because those were my favorite colors. We'd added regular toppings, like sprinkles and chocolate chips. Then there was the fudge Dad had brought home from Batts Confections. He had cut it up into eensy weensy little squares, and we'd piled them on top of the cupcakes.

"Knock knock," Talisa said.

"Who's there?" we asked back.

"Al," she said.

"Al who?"

"Al-most don't wanna eat this, because it looks so pretty!"

Then she took a big bite.

"And it tastes better than it looks!" she said.

It was cool to have Mom in my class because I got to show her things, like my desk, and the terrarium where we were growing moss for earth science.

"Just one more thing to show you," I said. "Wait here, I'll get it."

It was my Free Write story from last week. Mrs. Finkel had pinned it to the back board, at the very top. I couldn't reach it, so I pulled a chair over and stood on top of it, like a ladder.

"Here, let me help," Evie said, coming to my side.

"I've got it," I told her, reaching up. I had my story at my fingertips.

"Stella, I'm going to have to ask you to step off that chair," Mrs. Finkel called.

"Come on down, sweetheart," Mom said.

My cheeks heated up again, with the bad kind of embarrassment, and it got worse when

Joshua called out, "Get off that chair, Smella *sweetheart*."

"I said I'd help," Evie said. "Because I'm tall."

She reached up as I reached down.

I'm not exactly sure what happened next. Maybe Evie knocked into me. Maybe I knocked into her. Maybe we didn't knock into each other at all, and I just lost my balance. All I know is one second I was on the chair, bending down. And the next second the chair and I were both sideways on the floor. And in between those seconds there was a SMASH CRASH, and a scream.

It was ME screaming, because it hurt so much. More than anything had ever hurt before in my whole entire life. The hurting shot up from my ankle through my body to the tip of my head. I felt dizzy and before I even knew what was happening, I threw up. I'd never thrown up in school before. I was blushing and screaming and coughing and crying. Mom was suddenly at my side. So was Mrs. Finkel.

"Stella threw up," I heard Joshua say.

"That's enough," Mrs. Finkel said. Her voice was stern, even though he'd said *Stella* and not *Smella*, and what he'd said was exactly right. "Stand back, kids. Stand back. Go sit at your desks."

My right ankle hurt so bad. SOOOO BAD.

"Don't touch it," Mom said.

I didn't know I'd reached down to touch my ankle. I didn't know what I was doing at all. I was crying and crying, and then Mrs. Finkel said the scariest words I'd ever heard anyone say.

In a really low, really serious voice, she told Mom: "I think we need to call 9-1-1."

CHAPTER 4

More Bad Things

Mrs. Finkel had all the kids except me go across the hall to the other third-grade class, Mrs. Bower's class. I heard Joshua complaining about it, because he wanted to wait for the ambulance people to arrive. But my leg hurt so much, I didn't even care about what Joshua said.

Mom stayed by me, except when she went to the front of the room to get paper towels to wipe the throw up off my shirt. Mrs. Finkel went out to the hall to show the paramedics in.

"I didn't know I was going to be sick," I wailed.

"Sometimes when something hurts a lot, it can make you throw up," Mom said.

"It *does* hurt," I said.

"I know, baby."

"Is my leg broken?" I cried.

"Probably so," Mom said. She was holding my hand tight with one hand, and stroking my hair with the other. "Don't look, don't look," she said.

"Does it look really awful?"

"It'll be okay."

"What if it's not?" I asked. "What if it never is okay again in my whole entire life?"

"Of course it will be okay," Mom said. But her voice was shaky, so I knew she was scared, too.

A few minutes later, Mrs. Finkel came back in, along with two paramedics. They told me their names, but it was hard to listen, because I was too busy being scared and hurting a lot. Plus, I was embarrassed again. This time because there was still throw up on my shirt.

"I don't want them to see my shirt," I whispered to Mom.

"Don't worry," she said. "They deal with medical emergencies all the time. They've seen much worse."

Since I couldn't walk, they put me on a stretcher and carried me out. Even moving an eensy weensy tiny bit made my leg hurt worse. Mom climbed into the ambulance with me. I was mostly crying, but in between I said, "I can't hear the sirens."

"We turn them on when we need them,"

one of the paramedics told me.

But then we stopped. I guess maybe there was a red light up ahead, or something. I couldn't see since I was lying down in the back with no windows. There was the "whoop whoop" siren sound, and we started moving again.

It didn't take very long to get to the emergency room of Somers General Hospital. I stayed lying down as the paramedics pulled me out of the ambulance. Mom was right by my side, jogging to keep up as they rushed me in. I was transferred to a new bed. "Ow ow ow," I cried again, because every time they moved me, it hurt.

When I looked around, I saw three other kids in beds around the room. Two of them were also crying, and their parents were in chairs next to their beds, like Mom was right next to mine. But the third kid wasn't crying at all, and the chair next to her was empty.

I guess she wasn't hurt too badly. She didn't look hurt AT ALL. As a matter of fact, she looked perfectly healthy and well.

I wished I had whatever she had instead of what I did have. I would've clicked my heels together to make the wish, but I couldn't move my leg.

Just then a woman came by with a needle in her hand. I tried to scoot back in bed, away from her. But it's hard to scoot back when you have a probably-broken leg, and I cried out again.

"Hi, Stella, I'm Patricia," the woman said. "I'm a nurse here at Somers General, and I'm going to put in an IV. That'll help with your pain. Okay?"

"No, it's not okay," I said. "No IVs and no

needles. PLEASE! Mom, don't let her give me any needles!"

"I'm sorry, Stel," Mom said. "But I think you need it."

"You *do* need it," Patricia agreed. "We need to hook up an IV to get some pain medication into you. I bet that leg hurts a lot, doesn't it?"

I nodded miserably. Just thinking about how much my leg hurt made it hurt even more.

"The needle only goes in for a couple seconds, so I can pass something called a catheter through it," Patricia said. "That catheter will deliver your pain meds to make your leg feel better. As soon as the catheter is in, I'll take the needle out."

"That doesn't sound so bad, Stella," Mom said.

I looked at the needle and catheter in Patricia's hand. The needle looked just like you'd expect a needle to look. The catheter was white, and about the same width as one strand of a Pull 'n' Peel Twizzler. I've always liked Twizzlers, but right then I wasn't sure if I'd ever eat one again.

"I'll make you a deal," Patricia went on. "You can pick which arm we use. Any arm you want."

I looked up from Mom's shoulder. "*Any* arm I want?" I asked.

"A deal is a deal," Patricia said.

"All right," I said. I reached a hand toward Patricia and grabbed *her* arm. "This one!"

"You're very funny," she said.

I wasn't trying to be funny. Even if the needle was just for a couple seconds, it was STILL a needle, and I didn't want it. "It's My

Birthday Observed," I said to Mom.

"Oh, Stel," Mom said. "If I could I'd give you MY arm. But unfortunately you're going to have to take the needle yourself. The faster you give Patricia your arm, the faster this part is over with."

I was so busy worrying about my shot that I didn't see the girl come over—the same girl who hadn't been crying. She didn't come over alone. She had a pole with her. The pole had wheels, so she'd wheeled it over to my bedside. There was a long, thin tube hanging from the pole. The other end of it was attached to an IV in her arm.

"Camille, what are you doing here?" Patricia asked.

"I wanted to tell her it wasn't going to hurt that much," the girl said.

"Did you hear that, Stella?" Mom said.

I did hear it. But I didn't really believe it.

"Thank you for letting us know," Mom told her.

Patricia said she'd walk Camille back to her own bed. I watched her walk across the room with Camille. Then she walked back to Mom and me. She changed her gloves, and picked up the needle again.

"No, no," I said. "Please, no."

"Close your eyes," Patricia said. "I'll be done before you know it."

"Mom?" I asked.

"I'm right here, Stella," Mom said. "Close your eyes."

Mom held me. I could feel when Patricia tied a rubber thing around my left arm. Then she rubbed a spot on my arm with an alcohol wipe. There was a prick. "OW!" I said.

"Almost done," Patricia said.

"There, there," Mom said. "You're okay."

"All right, we're all done," Patricia said. I opened my eyes. She was putting some tape on my arm to keep the catheter in place. Even if it wasn't technically a needle, it still poked out of my skin, just the way a needle would. To be honest, it didn't really hurt, but I was still sad about it. Across the way, I saw Camille watching me. She gave a little smile. I turned back to Mom.

After that, Patricia got a portable X-ray to take a picture of my leg and make sure that it was broken. She handed Mom a bunch of forms to fill out. "A doctor will be with you soon," she said. Then she left to talk to other people.

I was starting to feel sleepy, even though it was the middle of the day. I closed my eyes, and I don't know how much time passed. Maybe a few minutes. Maybe an hour. When I opened my eyes again, Mom was sitting there, in the exact same spot, but she wasn't holding the forms anymore.

"Did the doctor come?" I asked.

"Not yet, sweetie."

"Patricia said the doctor would be here soon," I reminded her.

"I'm sure the doctors have a lot of patients to get to," Mom said.

"Isn't this an emergency?" I asked.

Mom nodded. "I can go ask the nurse."

"No, don't leave me."

So we waited some more. Finally a woman arrived. "Hello, I'm Dr. Marconi," she said. She turned to me. "You must be Stella."

"Yes," I said.

She pulled a curtain around my bed for privacy, and stuck some X-ray pictures up on a light board. "Well, Stella," she said. "You certainly did a good job breaking your leg."

"I didn't do it on purpose," I told her.

"Of course not," she said. She pointed to some of the jaggedy edges on the X-ray picture, and said something about a compound fracture of my left tibia, whatever that meant. It was all very confusing. Mom nodded like she understood. I was too tired to ask what all the words meant.

Outside the curtain, I heard someone say, "Excuse me. I'm looking for my daughter."

That made me feel more awake. "Daddy!" I cried.

The doctor pulled the curtain back open, and Dad came to my side. Mom was already holding my right hand. Dad reached for my left, but he had to hold it very carefully because that was the arm with the IV in it.

"Don't you have to be at work because

Stuart's not there?" I asked.

"Jessica and Claire are taking care of the store," he said, naming two more people who work at Batts Confections. "I have to be with YOU."

"What about Penny and Marco?" I asked.

"Mrs. Miller is with them," Dad said. "Don't worry. What about you—how are you?"

"Scared," I told him. And just saying that word made my eyes tear up an eensy weensy bit again.

"There's no need to be scared," Dr. Marconi said. "Do you know how many dozens of kids come in here with broken tibias? I've fixed them all up, good as new. You'll get an operation and—"

"An operation?" I broke in. "I don't want an operation."

"I'm afraid you need one," Dr. Marconi

said. "You'll stay here for a couple days, but don't worry—"

"But I can't stay here for a couple days," I broke in again. "I have to go to Pennsylvania tomorrow."

Mom, Dad, and Dr. Marconi shared looks with each other across my bed. The kind of looks grown-ups give each other when they think kids are too young to understand what's going on.

"How about if you just give me a cast, like other people get? And maybe crutches, too." Crutches would be fun to show Willa. "I think that's a good plan. My leg isn't even hurting so much anymore."

"The medication in the IV is why your leg doesn't hurt anymore," the doctor said.

"That's what Patricia said," Mom reminded me gently.

"But can't we *try* a cast and crutches?" I asked. "If I still need an operation, we can do it after I get back from Pennsylvania. That'll be on Tuesday."

The grown-ups gave each other more looks above my head. But even if they thought I was too young, I knew exactly what was going on.

"Oh no!" I cried. "My birthday is ruined!"

CHAPTER 5

All of a Sudden

All of a sudden I had a bunch of visitors. Patricia came back to take off my clothes and put me into a hospital gown. It sounds like it should be an easy thing to do, like taking off what you wore to school and changing into a nightgown at the end of the day. But when you have a compound fracture of your left tibia, it's not easy at all. Even with all the pain medicine and my leg in a splint, the nurse had to be really careful about moving me. Instead

of pulling my shorts off like normal, she CUT
THEM OFF.

Yes, you read that right! Patricia took
a pair of scissors and cut them right off me.
They were my favorites, too. Dad said don't
worry, I could get new ones. I didn't think he
was right about that though, because Mom
got them for me LAST summer. The store
probably didn't have the same ones anymore.

But I had bigger things to be upset about.
Like how I wasn't going to see Willa for my
birthday.

And the biggest upsetting thing of all:
THE OPERATION.

When my clothes were off and my gown
was on, Patricia put all my stuff in a plastic
bag and handed it to Mom, even my cut-off
shorts. They were ruined, but they went in the
bag, too.

My heart was pounding pounding POUNDING. Harder than when I accidentally cut too many bangs in my hair. Harder than when Penny, Lia, and I got locked in a hotel closet. Harder than when Joshua and I thought we saw a ghost on the library sleepover. Harder than it had ever pounded in my whole entire life.

"I don't want to have an operation," I said.

"I know, sweetheart," Mom said.

"You're going to be fine, darling," Dad added.

"That's right," Patricia said. "We have the best doctors in the world working here at Somers General. And they'll come to talk to you about it before you're wheeled in, so you will know exactly what to expect. Okay?"

I said, "Okay," but I didn't actually feel okay about it.

Patricia left, and my parents and I were waiting again. I never realized that the thing you do the most when you're in a hospital is wait.

"Can I use your cell phone to call Willa?" I asked.

Mom shook her head. "Sorry, sweets," she said. "There's a rule against cell phone calls in the emergency room."

"Why?"

"Because there are lots of medical machines in here," she said. "Sometimes making a phone call can interfere with the work the machines are doing. But you can play some games, if you want."

"Really?" I asked. Mom and Dad never let Penny and me play games on their phones, even though a lot of other parents let their kids. They think it's too much technology.

"Sure."

"But it's a rule that we can't," I reminded her.

"I think it's okay if we break that rule just this once, don't you?" Mom asked.

"Yeah, okay," I told her. Mom took her phone from her purse and handed it over. I played two and a half games of Pony Hair

Salon, and then two more people came in to talk to us. I was in the middle of braiding a palomino pony's hair with yellow and blue sparkle ribbons when Dad motioned for me to give Mom her cell phone back.

"Hello," the man said. He had on scrubs and a stethoscope around his neck. I knew he was a doctor, not a nurse, because his scrubs were blue like Dr. Marconi's, not the color of gummy Peachie O's, like Patricia's.

He picked up the chart that was at the edge of my bed and studied it for a couple seconds.

The woman who was with him wasn't dressed as a doctor or a nurse. She had on gray pants and a pink sweater and she said, "You must be Stella."

"Yes," I said.

"And Mr. and Mrs. Batts?"

"I'm Elaine," Mom told her.

"David," Dad said.

"I'm Mary Morrison. I'm a Child Life Specialist."

"You specialize in children's lives?" I asked.

"I specialize in helping kids who have to be in a hospital," she said.

The man put down my chart and introduced himself, too. His name was Dr. Fuentes and he was an anesthesiologist, which meant he was in charge of the medicine I'd get to put me to sleep for the operation, so I wouldn't feel a thing. He said he had a few questions for us, but mostly they were for Mom and Dad, about whether I'd ever had anesthesia before (I hadn't), and if I had any allergies (I didn't).

Mary Morrison had a bag with her, and she pulled an iPad out of it. When Dr. Fuentes was finished with his questions, she tapped on the iPad and turned it toward me to show me a picture of a white room with a bed in the middle and a bunch of machines around it. "This is what the operating room will look like," she told me. She swiped to the next picture. "And here is Dr. Marconi, who will be doing your operation."

"I met her," I said.

She showed me more pictures—one of Dr. Fuentes, who was still standing in the room with us, and then the nurse, Patricia, who'd cut off my shorts. The last picture she showed me was of three people with caps on their heads and masks on their faces. "This is what your doctors and nurse will look like when they put on their surgical caps and masks. You can tell the doctors apart because Dr. Marconi wears a plain surgical cap, but

Dr. Fuentes's has a jungle pattern on it."

"A very sophisticated jungle pattern," Dr. Fuentes said.

"I know they don't look like themselves," Mary Morrison went on. "But trust me, they're the same people under there. Okay?"

"Okay."

Mary Morrison put the iPad back in her bag, and pulled something else out. "This is the mask that you'll wear," she said.

The only time I'd ever worn a mask before was on Halloween. One time I was Spidergirl, and one time I was an owl. But this mask was much different from both of those. It was a see-through plastic circle that was big enough to fit over my nose and mouth. Mary Morrison gave it to me to hold. There was a tube coming out of the middle, and she told me that's where the gas would come in.

"Gas, like for a car?" I asked.

"A different kind of gas," she said. "This kind you breathe in, and it'll make you fall asleep, so you won't feel a thing during the operation. It may smell kind of funny, but I have something for you to take care of that."

She reached back down into her bag. You'll never guess what she pulled out so I'll just tell you. It was lip gloss! She had a bunch of different flavors: Banana Strawberry, Chocolate Milk, Vanilla Frosting, and Very Cherry.

"Pick the one you want," she told me.

"I have to wear lip gloss in my operation?" I asked. I glanced over at Mom. "You always tell Penny and me that we're too young for makeup."

"We can make an exception today," Mom said.

"Or not," Mary Morrison said. "You don't need to wear it if you don't want to."

"I do want to," I said.

"Okay," Mary Morrison said. "And we'll also rub the flavor you pick on the mask, so you'll smell the lip gloss instead of the gas."

She let me take the caps off all the lip glosses so I could smell them. I finally decided on Chocolate Milk, because it was the closest to smelling like chocolate fudge, which is my very favorite treat in the whole entire world.

Mary Morrison made a note about my lip gloss choice. Then she left, and so did Dr. Fuentes. Mom, Dad, and I were waiting again, but not for long, because Dr. Marconi came back. She drew an X on my broken leg with a black marker. She said it was so everyone knew what leg needed to be operated on.

There were papers for my parents to sign. Patricia was there and she flipped something on the bottom of my bed, and started to wheel me to the operating room. I was crying again. I couldn't help it. Mom's eyes were watery, like she was crying a little bit, too.

We rode in an elevator, and then down a long hall. Patricia said, "Okay, Stella, we need to say good-bye to your parents now."

"No!" I cried.

"It's only for a couple hours. You won't even feel the time passing, because you'll be asleep."

"Mommy," I said, crying more. I couldn't help it. It felt like saying good-bye forever. "Daddy!"

"I know, darling, I know," Dad said.

He clutched my hand. Mom kissed my cheeks and my forehead.

I was holding Dad's hands so tight, but he made me let go, so I grabbed on to Mom.

"It's okay," she said. "I'll be right here. So will Daddy. We'll be right here waiting."

Dad helped her peel my hands off hers. I saw him put an arm around Mom. Then I was wheeled through the double doors, and they were gone.

CHAPTER 6

The Signal

Dr. Fuentes and Dr. Marconi were already in the room when we got there. I could tell it was them from their surgical caps. Plus, there was another person, but I'd never seen him before. His surgical cap had little yellow ducks on it. He said his name was Peter. He had to be a nurse because his scrubs were the Peachie O's color, plus, he told me his first name, which I'd figured out doctors never did.

Patricia wheeled me up right beside the

operating table. She and Peter lifted me up very VERY carefully, and moved me over. The bed got wheeled away, and Dr. Fuentes stood in the space where it had been.

"Do you remember everything we talked about with Mary Morrison?" he asked me.

I was still crying a little bit, but I managed to nod.

"Chocolate Milk, right?" Peter asked, and I nodded again.

Dr. Fuentes lifted a mask, just like the one in Mary Morrison's bag, and moved to put it on my face.

"No, no, I'm not ready!" I said.

Patricia knelt beside me. Her face was so  close to mine, I could smell her breath: minty, like she'd just had one of the green mint sucking candies we have on the Penny Candy Wall at Batts Confections.

"It's all right, Stella," she said. "Dr. Fuentes is here to make sure you get all the medicine you need to fall asleep. Dr. Marconi will fix your leg. And Peter and I are here for you."

I looked over. Peter was right next to Dr. Fuentes, kneeling by me like Patricia was.

"We're here for you, Stella," Patricia said again. "We'll be here the whole time. We won't leave you."

"That's right," Peter said.

"What if I feel something and I can't talk because there's a mask on my face?" I asked.

"You won't feel a thing," Peter told me. "No one ever does."

"But what if I *do*?" I asked. "This could be the first time someone feels something in an operation."

"We can have a signal," Patricia said. "You

can raise your hand."

"My right hand," I told her. "There's an IV in my left arm and that hand is harder to raise."

"Your right hand," Patricia agreed.

"Like this," I said, and I raised my hand like I was in school and I knew the answer. I wished I were in school right then. Even though Mrs. Finkel was sometimes strict, I'd rather be with her than with all the doctors and nurses. I'd rather be anywhere else in the whole entire world!

"I'll stay here, on your right side, the whole time," Patricia said. "I'll look out for the signal. Okay?"

"Okay."

"But, Stella," Peter said, "I don't think you'll have to use it."

"It's good to have one just in case," I said.

"Sometimes you wake up when something hurts. Like one time my sister pulled my hair when I was asleep. I felt it, and it made me wake up."

"The medicine will keep you asleep," Peter said. "Don't worry."

"And I know the signal," Patricia said. She was speaking soft and low, just to me. And in that same voice she said, "Dr. Fuentes, I think we're ready now."

Dr. Fuentes put the mask on me. It smelled like chocolate milk. But under the chocolate milk smell, there was something else, too. Something that smelled like rotten eggs. I felt my eyes get hot with tears again.

"I hate this," I said, even though there was a mask over my mouth and it was hard to speak.

"Just breathe and count backwards in your head," Patricia told me. "Let's start at ten. By the time you get to one, I promise, you won't be awake anymore."

She counted out loud and I counted in my head. "Ten." I was still wide awake. "Nine." Awake. "Eight." Awake. "Seven. Six." Awake. Awake. "Five."

Patricia's voice got farther away, like she was speaking from across the street, or maybe down the block.

"Four."

I couldn't hear her anymore.

What number came next?

I couldn't remember.

Remember when?

CHAPTER 7

The Recovery Room

"*Five! Four! Three! Two! One!*" *Dr. Marconi shouted. She wasn't in her scrubs anymore. She was wearing a suit and a top hat.*

"*Okay, let's get this show started,*" *Dr. Fuentes said. I don't know why he was dressed like a gorilla.*

"*No, wait!*" *I cried. "I'm not asleep yet. I'm still awake. I'm still WIDE AWAKE!*"

"*Patricia, turn up the music, will you?*" *Dr. Marconi said. "I can't hear my cue.*"

Patricia didn't look like herself anymore. She looked like Willa. Except not the same size. No, this Willa was as small as a fairy you could cup in your hand, and she floated over to the DJ booth at the corner of the operating room. I hadn't noticed a DJ booth before.

"What's going on?" I asked Peter, who was right next to me. But he was wearing the gas mask, and he was sound asleep.

Some music started blasting. It was the Barbra Streisand show tunes that Grandma always played in the car, but the words were all wrong, like the way Penny would sing them.

The Willa-Patricia-fairy twirled up higher and higher until she floated into the sky. "Where are you going?" I asked.

"To Pennsylvania," she said, and she was gone.

"Let's get started," Dr. Fuentes said again.

"No! I'm still awake! And I don't even have Patricia with me anymore! She flew away and left me!"

Dr. Marconi took off her top hat and smeared Very Cherry lip gloss all over her lips. "Which leg is it again?"

"You get to pick," Dr. Fuentes said. "Hold on, I have a call."

Dr. Marconi did eeny meeny miny moe on my legs. Then she lifted my left leg and said, "I think I'll operate on this."

"NOOOOOOOOOOOO!!!!!!!" I cried.

"Phone for you," Dr. Fuentes the gorilla told Dr. Marconi, holding out a banana. Then he took my left leg in his big gorilla hands. "I'll take care of this," he said.

"Help me!" I said to Peter, but he just rolled over in his sleep.

I searched the sky for Patricia. I couldn't

see her, but I raised my right hand anyway. That was our signal. I raised it as high as I could and I waved it around and around. "I'm awake!" I cried. "Patricia, if you can hear me, I'm awake I'm awake I'm awake! WILLAAAAA!!!!!!!!!!!!"

Someone was speaking. I didn't recognize the voice, but she knew *me*. "I think Stella Batts is awake," she said.

"I know I'm awake!" I said. "That's what I've been trying to tell everyone!"

But my voice wasn't working and my eyes were closed. It was hard to open my eyes. Why was it so hard to open my eyes?

I tried my voice again. "Mmm mmm," I said.

"What was that, sweetheart?"

There were sounds all around—beeps

and blips, and footsteps, and things being wheeled around, and more voices.

I tried talking again. "Help me! Help!"

"There, there," the stranger said. There was a cool hand on my hand. "Your parents will be here soon. Don't worry. You're fine. Don't worry."

"I didn't fall asleep yet," I said. I opened my eyes, just a crack. Everything was fuzzy. "Don't let them start yet. I didn't fall asleep."

I tried to lift my other hand, the hand that wasn't being held, to wipe my eyes. But something hurt and pulled me back.

"Help!" I said. "I'm tied down!"

"Stella, it's okay," the voice said. A hand was on my forehead now.

"What's happening to me?" I cried.

"You still have the IV in. But the operation is all over. It went great."

"But I thought that . . . What happened to the doctors?"

"They did a great job on your leg."

Someone patted the corners of my eyes with a tissue. I blinked and blinked. "You're . . . ," I started. "You look just like . . ."

"I'm Joshua's mom," she supplied.

That was it! Joshua from my class—it was his mom! Mrs. Lewis! What was she doing there with me, after my operation? I wanted MY mom. And my dad. And my house, and my room, and all my things. And maybe also some fudge from the store.

"I'm a nurse," Mrs. Lewis told me. "And you're in the recovery room, where everyone comes after their operations. Another one of the nurses went to get your parents. They'll be here in a minute. In the meantime, I won't leave you."

My eyelids felt so heavy. I couldn't keep them open. I closed them again. Mrs. Lewis kept her hand on my forehead, smoothing back my hair. "The hard part is over," she said.

Then I heard my mom's voice. "Oh, Stella!"

And my dad's voice. "Hi, darling, we're right here."

I opened my eyes again, and I cried some more when I saw them. I don't think I'd cried so much in one day ever in my whole entire life. Well, maybe I did when I was a baby. Marco sometimes cries the whole day for no reason.

Unlike Marco, I had a reason. A big reason. I'd just broken my leg and had an operation and it was almost my birthday!

But I was tired again, so I went back to sleep.

CHAPTER 8

Out With a Smash

The next time I woke up, my eyes weren't so heavy. It was almost like waking up on a regular day.

Except on a regular day I'd be in my house, in my own bed. This bed was different. The sheets were white, and a little bit scratchy. The pillow wasn't soft. My pillow at home is squishy as a marshmallow. And the most different thing—at the end of the bed, my broken leg was propped up on a big piece of foam.

I turned my head. Dad was sitting in a chair, reading.

"Hi," I said.

He put his book down. "Oh, hi there, darling," he said, speaking softly. He leaned forward and pushed my bangs back from my eyes. "How are you feeling?"

"What time is it?" I asked.

Dad moved his hand from my forehead to check his watch. "Just about eight o'clock," he said.

"But it's still light out," I said, looking at the window behind him. "How is that possible?"

"It's not Friday anymore," he said. "You slept through the night. It's Saturday morning."

"Wow," I said. "That's so weird. When I fell asleep, I didn't know I was going to sleep for the whole night. Now I'm in a whole new day. I wonder if I missed anything."

"You missed a lot of Mom and me pacing around, waiting for your operation to be over," Dad said. "Then you fell back to sleep, and you missed being moved to this room, and the doctors getting your leg set up. You missed Mom kissing you good-bye."

"Oh no!" I said.

"Don't worry," Dad said. "She'll be back soon."

"Okay, good," I said. I shifted around in bed.

"Careful," Dad said. "Your leg is really fragile."

"I want to sit up," I said. "I can't sit up."

Dad reached over and pressed a button on the bedrail. It made the top half of my bed lift up. There, that was better.

There were more buttons on the railing. One was to call the nurses' station. (I pressed it by accident, and a nurse named Gina came in.) There was also a remote on a cord that I could pull up. It turned on the TV across from my bed, which had a bunch of channels, including a game channel that was even better than playing Pony Hair Salon.

Gina had peach scrubs on, just like Patricia and Peter, but she didn't have a mask or a surgical cap. "Well, good morning, Ms.

Batts," she said. "How about we take your vital signs while I'm here?"

I didn't know what vital signs were, but she told me: my blood pressure and my temperature. She said both were exactly what they were supposed to be, and she said my breakfast delivery would be in shortly.

"Delivery—like room service?" I asked.

There'd been a room service menu at the Hotel Aoife, where we'd stayed for Aunt Laura's wedding. But Penny and I didn't actually get to order anything, because we'd been busy with wedding stuff.

Now Gina opened a drawer in the cabinet next to my bed, and pulled out menus for lunch and dinner. "Your dad took care of your breakfast order," she told me. "But you can decide what you'll have next. Okay?"

"Okay!" I said.

"And Camille will be happy to hear you're awake," Gina said.

"Who's Camille?"

"Your roommate."

"I have a roommate?"

"You sure do," Gina said. "She's in the playroom now, but I'll tell her you're up."

"There's a playroom?"

Wow. Hospitals sure weren't like what I expected them to be.

"Unfortunately, Dr. Marconi doesn't want you moving that leg just yet, so you're not going to be able to go down there for a couple days. But we can bring some toys to you. Plus, it looks like you've already discovered your TV has a game channel."

"It looks really cool," I said. "But I can't do *everything* from my bed. Like, I'll still have to get up when I have to go to the bathroom."

"Don't you worry about that," Gina said. "When you have to go, I'll bring the bathroom to you."

I sort of had to go right then. Gina left and came back a couple minutes later with a piece of plastic that sort of looked like a toilet seat, and sort of looked like a bowl. Dad left the room to give me some privacy with Gina. She had me hook my arms around her neck, and oh-so-gently, she lifted me up so she could slide the plastic thing under me.

"It's hard to go when I'm not sitting on a real toilet," I said. "I hate this."

"I know," Gina said. "It'll get easier. Just relax. Close your eyes. Take a deep breath. You can do it."

I hated feeling like I had to go to the bathroom, but not be able to go. Finally I went. Gina cleaned me up. It was my last day of being eight, and I couldn't even go to the bathroom by myself. I felt like a baby, like my brother, Marco. Penny was wrong—it was not fun to be a baby again. Not at all!

But then Dad came back in, and someone delivered my breakfast. There was a table that slid over, so I could eat in  bed. After I was done, Mom came with Penny. My roommate, Camille, came back from the playroom and she said hello to everyone. She was the same girl I had seen earlier. She walked perfectly fine on her two unbroken legs. Her arms weren't broken, either. Nothing looked wrong with her. I wondered why she had to be at Somers General Hospital at all. I didn't ask because I knew it would be rude. But Penny is only five years old, so she didn't know.

"What's wrong with you?" she asked Camille.

"Penelope Jane!" Mom said. "That's not nice to ask."

"But no one has to ask Stella what's wrong with her, because you can see her bad leg," Penny said. "How else will I know if I don't ask?"

Which was exactly what I was thinking.

"I have diabetes. I just found out yesterday," Camille said.

Penny looked up at Mom. "Am I allowed to ask what that is?" she asked. "Because I don't know."

"It means I can't eat sugar," Camille explained.

"Are you allergic to sugar?" I asked.

"Stella's allergic to lettuce!" Penny exclaimed.

"No, she's not," Mom said.

"I wish I was so I never had to eat it," I said.

"Well, I'm not exactly allergic to sugar," Camille said. "My body just doesn't know what to do with it when I eat it. So I'm not allowed to have candy anymore."

"Not at all?" Penny asked. "Not even a SLIVER?"

Slivers are what we call the eensy weensy pieces of fudge you can get as free samples at Batts Confections.

"I don't know," Camille said. "But I don't think so."

"Wow," Penny said. "I don't know what I'd do if I couldn't eat sugar."

"I think you'd be fine," Dad told her.

"At least you can walk," I said.

"Yeah," Camille said. "At least I can do that."

"Your leg will get better," Mom reminded me. "And then you'll be able to walk again, too."

Grandma Dee and Grandpa Willie came

a few minutes later. My little side of the room was packed with people. There weren't enough chairs, but Camille said we could use the ones on her side.

"When your parents come, we'll give them back," Mom promised.

"I don't think they will," Camille said. "My mom doesn't live in California and my dad has to work."

"What's your dad's job?" Penny asked.

"He manages the supermarket by our house," Camille said.

"Can't he take the day off?"

"That's a lot of questions out of you, Penelope Jane," Mom told her.

"That's okay," Camille said. "I don't mind telling you. He can't. I mean, I guess he could, but then he wouldn't get paid."

"Oh," Penny said, and after that she was

just quiet. I guess she was out of questions.

But Dad had one. "Do you want to hang out with us for a little while?" he asked Camille.

"Sure," she said. "I can even bring some games back from the playroom."

"Goody!" Penny said. "Can I go and help pick them out?"

"If Camille says yes, then you can," Mom said.

Camille said yes. But when she and Penny got back, I was feeling tired, even though I hadn't been awake that long. Dad said I probably still had a lot of medicine in my system from when they put me to sleep for the operation. I needed a nap, which made me feel like baby Marco all over again.

Grandma and Grandpa said goodbye, and so did Dad and Penny. Camille walked around the curtain to her side of the room, and Mom sat next to me with a book, while I closed my eyes.

ZZZZZZZZZZZZZZZZZZZZZZZZZZZZ
That's me napping.
ZZZZZZZZZZZZZZZZZZZZZZZZZZZZ

When I woke up, Mom said Aunt Laura had texted and wanted to talk to me. We called her on FaceTime. She was with Uncle Rob, and Lia, too. Everyone wanted to see my broken leg. I moved the phone to give them a glimpse.

"Wow," Uncle Rob said. "Looks like age eight is going out with a bang."

"More like a smash," I told him.

"Feel better, Stella," Lia said.

When we hung up, Mom let me call

Willa, but she wasn't home. I left a message.

"Hi, Willa," I said. "I should be with you right now, planning my birthday dinner, but instead I'm in this stupid hospital. Call me back, okay? Thank you. Oh, this is Stella by the way."

And then I called Evie. "Stella!" she said. "Are you okay? I've been so worried about you!"

"I'm in the hospital," I told her. "My leg is broken and I had an operation, so I can't go to Pennsylvania."

"I know," she said. "My mum told me. She said you were in the same hospital where I got my stitches."

"Yes, but you didn't have to sleep over, did you?"

"No," Evie said. "I only had seven stitches."

"I don't know how many I had, but probably a lot more," I said. "And I have to stay here even though it'll be my birthday tomorrow. Do you think you could come visit?"

"Um . . . ," she said. "I don't know. I think my parents said I'd be busy tomorrow."

"Well, can you ask them?"

"Yeah, okay," she said. "But I think they'll say no."

We said good-bye, and I handed Mom back her phone. "You only turn nine years old once in your whole entire life," I told her. "Now I'll never get to make it a good birthday. This was my one chance, and my one chance is over."

"It's not your birthday yet, sweetheart," Mom said. "Anything can happen."

"Do you think my leg will be better by then, because Dr. Marconi said no."

"I'm afraid Dr. Marconi is right about that," she said. "But let's focus on the good things."

"There are no good things," I told her. "I'm tired again."

I closed my eyes and went back to sleep.

CHAPTER 9

Officially Nine

I woke up in the middle of the night.

"Mom?" I said.

But Mom wasn't there. The chair beside my bed was empty. The big lights were off. There was light coming in through the window, and also from down the hall, so I could see a little bit around me. I could see Mom's purse on the chair, and the blanket scrunched up on the footstool.

She wouldn't have left her purse if she

was leaving me. Maybe she was just in the bathroom. I started to count in my head as I waited for her. I counted all the way up to three hundred. It takes about three hundred seconds to count up to the number three hundred. That equals five minutes. What was taking Mom so long?

I started to cry a little bit, but not too hard, because I heard footsteps coming closer, which meant Mom was coming back.

"Where were you?" I started to say. But then I stopped myself, because it wasn't Mom who came around from the other side of the curtain. It was Camille.

"Does your leg hurt?" she asked.

"No," I said.

"Oh," she said. "I heard you crying, so I thought maybe it was hurting you. I could call a nurse, if you want."

"It's okay," I said. I sniffled and wiped my eyes with my hand that didn't have the IV in it. "I just don't know where my mom went. I'm sorry if I woke you up."

"Oh, don't worry. I was awake anyway," Camille said. "It's hard to sleep in here."

"Yeah," I said. "It's okay when my mom is here—or my dad."

"My dad has to be home at night for my sister," Camille said.

"You have a sister?"

"Yeah, her name is Lexi. She's three."

"So you, your dad, and your sister live in California," I said.

"Yup," Camille said. "And my mom lives in Pennsylvania, which is two thousand and eight hundred miles away. I looked it up."

"I was supposed to take a plane to Pennsylvania today," I said. "Tomorrow is my

birthday, so that's why. I wonder if my friend Willa knows your mom."

"Maybe," Camille said.

"What's her name?"

"Tabitha," Camille said. "Why?"

"I'm going to ask Willa if she knows her," I said.

"There are a lot of people who live there," Camille said. "I bet she doesn't."

"Yeah," I said. "You're probably right."

We were both quiet, and the quiet part

seemed to go on for a long time. It was Camille's turn to talk, but she didn't say anything. She just watched me, and I watched her.

Finally I said something. "You can go back to bed if you're tired," I told her.

"I'm not tired," she said. "But I'll go back if you are."

I shook my head. "I'm not tired, either," I said. "Do you still have those games from the playroom? I'll play with you now, if you want."

"No," Camille said. "But I do have something. I'll be right back."

She went around the curtain to her side of the room, and came back with a plain deck of cards, which is all you need to play the best game in the world. If you've read my other books, you can probably guess what it is. But if you can't, that's okay, because I'll just tell you . . .

SPIT!!!!!!!

I don't know why it's called Spit, because it has nothing to do with saliva. But that's the name of the game. I asked Camille if she knew how to play it.

"Of course I do," she said. "That's why I have the cards in my backpack. My friends and I play at lunch sometimes."

"That's so funny," I said. "Because MY friends and I play at lunch sometimes, too."

Camille sat across from me on my bed, next to my good leg, not my bad one. She slid my table between us and split the deck. I took my half of the cards, and we each made our five piles. "One, two, three, spit!" she said.

I flipped over one of my cards, she flipped over one of hers, and after that it went really

fast. We finished the round in record time. Camille won, so she picked the smaller pile, since the goal of Spit is to have fewer and fewer cards until you're left with none.

We dealt out the cards for round two. "Ready?" I asked, reaching for a Spit card.

"In a sec," Camille said, straightening her piles. "Happy birthday, by the way," she said.

"Not till tomorrow," I reminded her.

"I think it's probably tomorrow right now," she said. "It's pretty late."

"That makes you the first person to wish

me happy birthday on my actual birthday," I told her. She smiled. "When's your birthday?"

"In six months," Camille said.

"What's the date?" I asked.

"November twenty-first," she said.

"That's my half birthday," I said. I paused. "Wait a second. That means MY birthday is YOUR half birthday!"

"Yes, I told you it's in six months," she said.

"But I didn't know you meant EXACTLY six months," I said. "We're kind of twins. My birthday is your half, and your birthday is mine. Plus, we're both here, and we're both good at Spit."

"Speaking of Spit," she said, "I'm ready now."

"One, two, three, spit!" we said together, and we started round two.

We played even faster than the last time. At first it looked like Camille would win the round again, but then I started winning, and then—

"Girls!"

"Mom!" I said. "What are you doing here?"

"What am I doing here?" she repeated. "I'm staying here—because YOU are staying here."

"Oh, right," I said. "I forgot for a second. You see, I woke up and I didn't know where you were. I got really scared and I started to cry a little bit."

"I'm sorry, Stel," Mom said.

"It's okay," I told her. "Camille heard me and she came over to keep me company. Then we were having fun so I forgot we were at a hospital in the middle of the night, because it felt a little bit like a playdate."

Mom smiled. "Thank you for being here, Camille," she said.

"You're welcome," Camille said.

"I'm glad you were here for my girl, but now you both need to get some rest."

"It's hard to rest when you don't have a grown-up," I told Mom.

"I know, sweets," she said. "Camille, would you like me to get a nurse to sit with you while you fall asleep, and I'll sit with Stella?"

"Yes, please," Camille said.

Mom went out for a minute, and came back in with Gina. Gina pulled Camille's IV pole as Camille walked back to the other side of the curtain. "Wait," she said. "Is it Sunday yet?"

Gina looked at her watch. "As a matter of

fact, it is. Just now. It's midnight."

"Happy birthday!" Camille told me.

"Shhh," Gina said gently. Then she added, "Happy birthday, Stella."

"Thanks," I said. "Hey, Camille, happy *half* birthday to you."

"Thank you," she said.

She disappeared behind the curtain. I could hear Gina getting her settled into bed, while Mom sat back down on her chair and propped her feet up on the footstool, which was a little bit like lying down.

"What time was I born?" I asked Mom.

"Just about four o'clock in the morning," she said, talking softly, so she wouldn't disturb Camille on the other side of the curtain.

"So it's not really my birthday yet."

"Almost," Mom said. "Exactly nine years ago to this very second, I was a couple floors down in this very hospital, getting ready to meet you for the first time."

"Tell me what happened," I said.

I'd heard the story before, but I wanted to hear it again. The story of when I was born is one of my favorites. I also like stories about when I was a baby, because I can't remember them, but I'm still in them.

"Daddy and I got to the hospital, and we didn't know if you were going to be a boy or a girl," Mom said. "Since you were our first baby, we wanted it to be a surprise. We had names all picked out—Andrew for a boy, and Nicole for a girl."

"And then I was born, and the doctor said, 'It's a girl!'"

"Shush," Mom said, but she was smiling. "Yes, you were a girl," she said. "Our sweet baby girl. The most perfect baby your dad and

I had ever seen, and we fell in love with you instantly. There was just one problem."

"I didn't look like a Nicole," I whispered.

"The way a chocolate doesn't look like a gummy."

Mom smiled. "Exactly," she said. "We still loved the name, but it wasn't quite right for you. One of the nurses gave us a baby name book, and we tried out all different names for you, but none of them fit. Then the morning after you were born you were being fussy, and your dad said, 'Sweet dreams, little Stella.' I remembered the name from the book I'd loved when I was just about your age, but I hadn't heard it since. You stopped crying right then, and Dad and I looked at each other. We agreed that was your name. You were a Stella. You are a Stella. Our Stella."

I smiled, feeling like I could almost

remember that moment myself. "Remember when I changed my name this year, and then I changed it back?"

"Of course I remember," Mom said. "You've had a lot of adventures this year."

"I cut my hair really short," I said. "Willa moved away, and I met Evie. I was in a wedding, and I got a new cousin. I got a pet fish. I was on TV."

Mom smoothed my hair back from my forehead. "Lots of good eight-year-old memories," she said. "I know nine isn't starting out the way you expected it to. But we'll do our best to make it a special birthday anyway."

"I don't want a cake," I said.

"You don't have to have anything you don't want," Mom said. "But may I ask why?"

I turned to look at the curtain, and then I looked back at Mom. In the softest whisper I'd ever whispered in my whole entire life, I said, "I don't want to have cake in front of Camille."

"I see," Mom said.

"Plus, it's her half birthday," I added.

"Okay, Stel," Mom said. "Don't worry."

"But really, Mom," I said. "It wouldn't be fair."

"Shhh," she said. "It's okay. I've got it. Go to sleep now. Have sweet dreams, little Stella."

"I'm not so little anymore," I reminded her.

"You'll always be little to me," Mom said. "My sweet birthday girl. Close your eyes now."

I had more to say, but my eyelids suddenly felt heavy. I closed my eyes, and fell asleep, and dreamed about birthday cakes all night long.

CHAPTER 10

Happy Birthday

When I woke up the next day, it really was my birthday. Even though I was in a hospital room, it LOOKED like my birthday. There were signs up that said, "HAPPY BIRTHDAY, STELLA!" in all the colors of the rainbow. There were balloons, too. Some regular balloons in yellow and blue, which are my two favorite colors. And then there were other balloons that looked like doctors' gloves, but all blown up.

Mom was in her chair beside me, looking out the window. "Mom," I whispered. "Mom!"

"Good morning, birthday girl," she said. She stood and came to the side of my bed. "Did you sleep well?"

"Yeah," I said. "I didn't even hear anyone come in to decorate. Was it you?"

She shook her head. "The hospital has little elves for that kind of thing," she said. "Like Christmas elves, but for birthdays. Do you like it?"

"I love it," I said.

"Is that Stella?" Camille called from the other side of the curtain. "Stella, you're awake?"

"I am!" I called back. "Come over!"

Camille came over, tugging her IV pole. "Happy birthday!" she said.

"Thanks," I said. "Happy *half* birthday to you!"

"Thanks," she grinned. "Do you like the signs?"

"I love them," I said.

"I made that one," Camille told me, pointing to the rainbow-est one of all, above the TV. "I got up extra early so it'd be a surprise."

"That's my favorite one!" I told her.

Gina came into the room to say happy birthday, and also to do hospital things, like take vital signs. Mom brought a little tray over, so I could brush my teeth. I rinsed and spit into a little bowl because the sink was too far away. Then I had to go to the bathroom. Camille went back to her side of the room, and Gina pulled the curtain. It wasn't as bad as the last time. But still, I told Gina I couldn't wait until I was allowed out of my bed.

Once I was all cleaned up, Gina pulled back the curtain between Camille's and my bed, so it was like we were in one big room. Breakfast was delivered. There was a candle in my pancakes. I made a wish and blew it out.

Camille had scrambled eggs to eat. I offered her a bite of my pancakes, but Gina said no because of the syrup. I felt bad eating

them in front of her. It made me a little bit less hungry, and I pushed the pieces of pancake around on my plate.

"Everything okay, Stella?" Mom asked.

I nodded. "Yeah, I just hope my wish comes true," I said.

"What'd you wish for?" Camille asked.

"I can't tell you," I said.

"Well, I hope it comes true, too," Mom said, bending down to kiss my forehead.

I looked over at Camille. "Hey, Mom, do you know what the lunch choices are yet?"

"I have the menu right here," she said. She read from the list: "A burger, spaghetti and meatballs, chicken nuggets, pizza, or peanut butter and jelly."

"What are YOU getting?" I asked Camille.

"I have a special menu," she said. "I picked a turkey hot dog."

"Do you think I can have the same thing?" I asked Mom.

"I'll let Gina know," Mom said.

"Thanks," I said. "And can you also ask if she can still bring me art supplies from the playroom?"

"I'm sure she would," Mom said. "You're in the mood to draw something today?"

"Yes!" I said. "I need to make *half* birthday signs to decorate Camille's side of the room!"

"Really?" Camille asked.

"Of course," I told her.

"That's an art project I'd like in on," Mom said. She went to talk to Gina, and came back with supplies. The three of us got to work. Our room had to be the most festive room in the whole entire hospital. When we were done, we started a Spit tournament, which went on for a long time because we're both really good

players. We played all the way up until it was lunchtime.

Camille went into the bathroom to wash her hands. Since I couldn't leave my bed, Mom gave me a wet nap.

"You remember what I said about the cake, right?" I asked.

"I do," Mom said.

"Okay, good." I paused. "You know what's weird? No one has visited me yet today."

"You had a lot of visitors yesterday," Mom reminded me.

"I know," I said. "But today's my birthday."

"Are you having an okay day?"

"Oh yes," I said. "And you want to know something?"

"What?"

"I sort of want visitors, but I sort of don't," I said, lowering my voice to a whisper. "I don't want Camille to feel bad."

"You're a sweet girl, Stella," Mom said.

"Unless my wish comes true," I said. "And then visitors would be okay."

Mom didn't get a chance to ask me about my wish, because Camille came out of the bathroom. Besides I wouldn't have told her, because when you tell wishes, there's a better chance that they won't come true.

After lunch, my wish didn't come true, but I did get a bunch of visitors. First Dad and Penny arrived. They didn't have Marco with them—he'd stayed behind with Mrs. Miller.

But they had MORE balloons. I told Dad to tie them up to the side of Camille's bed, since I already had a bunch. Then Grandma and Grandpa stopped by. They sat in Camille's guest chairs again. We didn't have to pull them over because the curtain was still open like one big room with everyone together. With all the decorations, it felt like a party.

Plus, there were presents. I got a big cozy stuffed animal from my grandparents. I thought I was a little bit too old for a stuffed animal.

But this one was special because you could use it as a pillow, too. Penny gave me a notebook with a dolphin on it. Dolphins are my favorite animal in the whole entire world, and notebooks are my favorite present, because I can write more books in them. "Thanks," I told her.

"Mom and I have a present for you, too," Dad said. "It just hasn't arrived yet."

"Wow," Camille said. "You're getting so much stuff."

My eyes slid to Camille, and then back to Dad. "That's okay," I said. "I don't need anything."

"I don't know what's in the hospital food," Dad said. "That doesn't sound like the Stella I know."

I felt my cheeks getting pink like cotton candy. Actually, they were hot enough that they may have been red as Swedish Fish candy. I was a little bit relieved when Grandma and Grandpa said they had to leave, even though Penny wasn't happy about it.

"You just got here," she said, pouting.

"I know, sweets," Grandma said. "But we have to go watch your brother. Mrs. Miller has plans this afternoon."

"You can come with us, if you want," Grandpa offered.

"But I don't want to . . ." Penny lowered her voice. "I don't want to miss the surprise," she whispered.

"It's not a cake, is it?" I said.

"Guess again!" Penny cried.

"That's enough out of you," Dad told her.

Then Grandma and Grandpa said they really had to go, so Penny ran over and gave them hugs good-bye. Of course I couldn't get out of bed to do the same, but they both leaned over the bed to say good-bye to me. Then they said good-bye to Dad.

"Where's Mom?" I asked. "She was just here a minute ago."

"I'm sure she'll be right back," Dad said.

"Good-bye, good-bye," Grandma and Grandpa called. As they walked out, I heard someone in the hall say, "Pardon me." I knew exactly who that was.

"EVIE!" I practically shouted.

Evie rushed into my room. Her dad was right behind her. "Happy birthday, Stella!" Evie said. "Oh my, you have quite a broken leg, don't you?"

"I do," I said. "I needed way more than seven stitches. The doctor didn't even count."

"Wow," she said.

I introduced Camille to Evie and her dad. They

all said *Nice to meet you* to each other. "I don't have a present for you yet, because Sara and Tesa are sending it from London," Evie explained to me. "I didn't think I'd see you until AFTER your birthday."

"That's okay," I said. "I'm glad you're here."

"Really? I thought you wanted to be with Willa."

"Hold that thought," Dad said.

Mom was walking back in the room. And she wasn't alone.

CHAPTER 11

My Birthday Wish

WILLA WAS WITH HER!!!!

Willa, plus her mom, whose name is Gayle. But I barely said hello to her. I just shouted: "WILLA!!!!!!!!"

"Welcome back to Somers, Willa Go-Getter," Dad said.

Penny was hopping up and down. "Do you like your surprise?" she asked me. "Do you like it?"

"I love it!" I said.

I wished I could jump up and give Willa the biggest hug in the whole entire world, but of course that wasn't possible. Instead, she leaned over my bed and we hugged with me propped against the pillows. Then she hugged my dad and Penny. (I bet she'd hugged my mom out in the hallway.)

Gayle hugged me and the rest of my family, too, and all the people who didn't know each other shook hands. I kept squeezing my eyes shut and opening them again to make sure the whole thing wasn't a dream, like when Dr. Fuentes was dressed like a gorilla. But every time I opened my eyes, Willa was STILL there! This was REAL LIFE!

"Stella, are your eyes okay?" Mom asked.

"Oh, yes," I told her. "They're fine. They just don't quite believe they're seeing the best surprise in the whole entire world!"

"I have more surprises for you," Willa said. She grabbed a bag her mom was holding, and brought out a big box. I pulled off the wrapping paper. You probably won't be able to guess what it was, so I'll just tell you:

A friendship bracelet–making kit!

"Now we can make matching ones!" Willa said.

"Thanks," I told her. "I'm going to make a whole bunch—one for you, and one for Camille, and one for Evie."

"For me?" Evie asked.

Right then I remem-
bered what had happened in
the car on the way to school
on My Birthday Observed. When I started talking about Willa, Dad changed the subject and said we'd talk later. I'd been so busy thinking about Willa that I hadn't

139

realized what he wanted to talk about, but now I did. Dad was worried I'd been hurting Evie's feelings.

Willa and I had been friends for a long time, and I missed her. But Evie was one of my very best friends, too. I would never want to say anything to hurt her.

"Yes, of course," I told her. "I'm really glad you're my friend."

"I'm glad you're mine, too."

"Batts Confections delivery!" someone called from the doorway. I looked over, and there was Stuart. "Delivery! For the eldest young Ms. Batts!"

"That's me," I said. "But I thought you didn't work at the store anymore."

"This is my last day," Stuart said. "I'd never move to New York before your birthday."

"Wow, thanks," I said.

He had a big Batts Confections bag with him—pink with silver writing that had BATTS CONFECTIONS written out in swirly letters. He reached in and pulled out—a cake! He placed it on the wheelie table right next to the bed, so I could look at it.

It was definitely the most beautiful cake I'd ever seen in my whole entire life—even more beautiful than the one we'd brought to Aunt Laura's wedding. That cake had five tiers, all decorated with different candy. This cake was only one tier, covered in yellow frosting. There were waves of blue frosting around the edges, and a frosting dolphin leaping across

the top of the cake. It had a sign in its mouth that said: HAPPY BIRTHDAY TO STELLA THE BRAVE!

"Stuart spent all night on it," Dad said. "What do you think?"

I thought it was greatest cake in the whole entire world.

But I also thought it was sad, because Camille couldn't eat it.

"I love it," I said. "Thanks, Stuart. Can we

put it back in the bag? I'd like to save it for later."

"Do you mean we don't get to eat cake right now?" Penny asked.

I shook my head.

"No fair!" she said.

"Are you not feeling well, darling?" Dad asked.

"No, I feel fine," I said. "I just don't feel hungry for cake."

That wasn't true, of course. I am ALWAYS hungry for cake, and I was especially right then. My stomach even grumbled a little, because the smell of cake deliciousness was making me even hungrier!

"If I'm hungry for cake, can I have a piece?" Penny asked.

"We're not cutting into your sister's birthday cake until she's ready," Dad said.

"Just a sliver?" Penny asked.

But Dad told Penny no—the cake would not be cut into until the birthday girl was ready. It was the Birthday Rule.

"Wah!" Penny fake cried.

"I think I know why Stella isn't hungry right now, and I may be able to fix that," Mom said. She leaned in close to me. "Stel, I want to assure you that everyone in this room is allowed to eat that cake."

"But . . . ," I started. I lowered my voice. "But the sugar," I nearly whispered.

"Your mom told me you wanted a sugar-free cake, and your birthday wish was my command," Stuart said.

"Really?"

"Yes, really," Mom said. "Plus, it's nut-free, so Willa can eat it, too."

I'd nearly forgotten about all of Willa's

allergies. "Hooray!" I said. "Happy birthday to me!"

"Goody!" Penny said. "Now we can eat!"

But Stuart said there was one more thing to do. He stuck ten candles in the cake—nine for my birthday, and one to grow on. Then he started to light them with a match.

"Wait!" Evie called out. She grabbed her dad's cell phone and punched some numbers in.

"Who are you calling?" I asked.

"You'll see," she said. She had the phone pressed against her ear. Someone must've picked up because she said, "Hi, it's Evie. Are you both there? Okay, good. I'm going to put you on speakerphone." She pressed a button, and held the phone out. Then she nodded to Stuart. "We're ready now."

He lit the candles, and everyone in the

room started to sing the happy birthday song, plus the people on the phone. I recognized Lucy's, Talisa's, and Arielle's voices.

"Happy birthday, dear Stella!" everyone sang. "Happy birthday to you!"

"Thank you," I said. I looked at Evie. "How did you know Lucy, Talisa, and Arielle would be all together?"

"We planned it," Evie said. "They wanted to be here too, but the hospital doesn't allow that many visitors all at once."

"Knock knock," Talisa said.

"Who's there?" I asked.

"Cards," she said.

"Cards who?"

"Cards we made you for your birthday because we couldn't be there! Evie said she'd bring them to you."

Talisa is always telling knock-knock jokes. Sometimes she makes them up and they don't make much sense. But this one made me smile.

"Everyone made cards," Arielle said softly. "Not just us. The whole class did after you left on Friday. We were all thinking about you and worrying about you. We couldn't concentrate on any school stuff, so Mrs. Finkel let us make cards instead."

"Even Joshua made one," Lucy said.

"Even Mrs. Finkel!" Talisa told me.

"I brought them all," Evie said. "Do you want them?"

"Oh yes," I said.

"Oh no!" Penny cried.

"No?"

"I mean not yet," she said. "First you need to make a wish and blow out your candles. And you need to hurry up! The wax is dripping on the frosting!"

"Oh, right," I said. "But I made a wish this morning. And I've gotten so many presents, I don't have any wishes left. But today is also Camille's *half* birthday, so she can make a wish this time."

Camille grinned and stepped up beside the cake. "I wish—" she started.

"Don't say it out loud," I warned her. "It needs to be a secret so it can come true."

She nodded and closed her eyes. I watched her lips moving slightly as she said her wish to herself. Then her eyes popped open. "Okay, let's blow the candles out together," she said.

We each inhaled a deep breath and BLEEEEEEEEEEEW out the candles—all ten of them. Camille and I pulled out the candles and licked the frosting off the bottoms. Then Dad took the cake away to cut it. "I have a first piece for the birthday girl," he said. "And a second piece for the half-birthday girl, and a third—"

"Excuse me," a man said, walking into the room. "I'm looking for my—"

"DAD!!!!!" Camille shouted.

I watched Camille cross the room, pulling her IV pole along before she jumped into her dad's arms. I could tell she was crying because her back was shaking. But it was the happy kind of crying. I felt my eyes get wet, too.

Camille pulled her dad over to my bedside, and we shook hands. He told me his name was Ed Markley. "It's nice to meet you, Mr. Markley," I said. "I'm so glad you came because it made my wish come true."

"You wished MY dad would visit you?" Camille asked. "Why? You already had so many visitors!"

"I know," I said. "That's why I wished it—because I wanted you to have a visitor, too."

"That's so sweet of you, Stella," Mom said. "I'm proud of you. You really are a grown-up nine-year-old girl."

I nodded, smiling. "I feel nine," I told her. "What about you, Camille? Do you feel nine and a half?"

"Oh, yeah, definitely," Camille said. "Before now, I'd never stayed the night without parents."

"I'm sorry you've been here on your own," Mr. Markley said.

"Well, I wasn't completely on my own," Camille said. "I had Stella."

"And I had Camille," I added. "We had each other."

"That's great to hear," Mr. Markley said. "And are you ready for more great news?"

"Oh yes!"

"The doctor said you get to come home today! Just as soon as you finish up the celebration in here, we can go. Lexi is off on a playdate this morning. Imagine how happy she'll be when we pick her up—together."

Camille let out a whoop. "Was that your half-birthday wish?" Penny asked. "Did it just come true?"

Camille shook her head. "Nope," she said.

"Oh, did you wish the same thing as Stella?"

"No, not that, either. I wished my dad would have a different job, so he could take a break if he needs to see me."

"Oh no!" Penny said. "You said your wish out loud!"

"You're the one who was asking her all about her wish," I told Penny.

"I'm sorry," Penny said, and she looked like she was going to cry, too—and not the happy kind of tears. "I didn't mean it. I take it back."

"That's okay," Camille said. "I didn't expect it to come true anyway."

"Well, I don't know about that," Dad said. "Because with Stuart leaving, I do need a new manager at Batts Confections, and I heard from your daughter yesterday that you have management experience."

"No kidding?" Camille's dad said.

"I'm not kidding at all," said Dad. "Why don't you come in tomorrow and I can show you the ropes."

"Do you know what this means?" I asked Camille.

"My wish came true?"

"That," I said. "And—we'll get to see each other a whole lot more! And it won't be in the hospital anymore!"

"Thank you," Mr. Markley said to Dad, and they shook hands.

"Thank you," Camille said, too.

"Yeah, Dad," I said. "Thanks. Thanks so much."

I wished I could get out of bed and leap up

and hug him the way Camille had hugged her dad. But of course I couldn't. Not right then, anyway. Sometimes wishes come true. Sometimes they take a long time. And sometimes you have wishes that aren't really possible at all, but that's okay, because other things come true instead. I had my family with me, and my old best friend, and my new one, and a brand-new friend, all celebrating my birthday with me. I had this feeling inside me that was so big, it was making me smile and cry at the same time. I didn't want to just hug Dad. I wanted to hug the whole world.

"Are you okay, Stella?" Penny asked.

"Yes, I am," I said. "I'm great. In fact, I need to make friendship bracelets for everyone!"

"Everyone?" Willa said.

"You can never have enough friendship bracelets, right, Dad?" I asked.

Dad winked at me. "That's right, darling."
"Well, we better get started," Willa said.
And so we did.

Courtney Sheinmel

Courtney Sheinmel has authored over a dozen highly celebrated books for kids and teens, including the Stella Batts series for young readers, the YA novel, *Edgewater*, and the middle-grade series, The Kindness Club. Like Stella Batts, Courtney was born in California and has a younger sister. Unlike Stella, her parents never owned a candy store. Courtney lives in New York City. You can visit her online at www.courtneysheinmel.com.

Jennifer A. Bell

Jennifer A. Bell is an illustrator whose work can be found on greeting cards, in magazines, and in more than two dozen children's books. After several years of living in Minneapolis, Minnesota, she recently relocated to Toronto, where she lives with her husband and cranky cat. Visit her online at www.JenniferABell.com.

Praise for Stella Batts

"Sheinmel has a great ear for the dialogue and concerns of eight-year-old girls. Bell's artwork is breezy and light, reflecting the overall tone of the book. This would be a good choice for fans of Barbara Park's 'Junie B. Jones' books."

— *School Library Journal*

"First in a series featuring eight-year-old Stella, Sheinmel's unassuming story, cheerily illustrated by Bell, is a reliable read for those first encountering chapter books. With a light touch, Sheinmel persuasively conveys elementary school dynamics; readers may recognize some of their own inflated reactions to small mortifications in likeable Stella, while descriptions of unique candy confections are mouth-watering."

— *Publishers Weekly*

"Why five stars? Because any book that can make a reader out of a child deserves five stars in my book! It's all about getting kids 'hooked' on reading."

— Pam Kramer, Examiner.com

"My daughter is nine years old and struggled with reading since kindergarten. Recently we found the Stella Batts books and she has fallen in love with them. She has proudly read them all and she can't wait till #6. We can't thank you enough. Her confidence with reading has improved 100%. It brings tears to my eyes to see her excited about reading. Thanks."

— K.M. Anchorage, Alaska

Meet Stella and friends online
at www.stellabatts.com

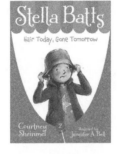

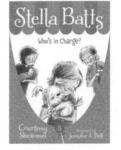

Other books in this series:

★ Stella Batts Needs A New Name

★ Stella Batts Hair Today, Gone Tomorrow

★ Stella Batts Pardon Me

★ Stella Batts A Case of the Meanies

★ Stella Batts Who's in Charge?

★ Stella Batts Something Blue

★ Stella Batts None of Your Beeswax

★ Stella Batts Superstar

★ Stella Batts Scaredy Cat